little Miss Twins

by Roger Hargreaves

D0522712

You just couldn't tell them apart!

Who?

Why, little Miss Twin and little Miss Twin of course!

Who did you think?

They lived in a funny sort of a country called Twoland.

Why was it called Twoland?

You'll find out soon enough!

One morning little Miss Twin and little Miss Twin were having breakfast.

Two boiled eggs each!

Suddenly, there were two knocks at the door.

They both went to see who it was.

And there, standing on the doorstep, were two postmen!

"Good morning morning," they said.

People in Twoland tended to talk like that!

"Two letters for you you," they said.

"Oh good good," exclaimed the twins.

They read their letters while they finished breakfast.

After reading their letters, and after washing up, and after making their twin beds, the twins went shopping.

To Twotown!

On the way they passed two policemen.

"Hello hello," they said.

The twins bought two loaves of bread from Mrs Twiceslice, the baker's wife.

Then they went into Mr Doublechop the butcher's, and bought some sausages.

"Two pounds of your very best sausages please please," they said.

"You'll enjoy these these," smiled Mr Doublechop, as he wrapped up the sausages.

In two parcels!

Then the twins went home to Twotimes Cottage.

Oh, didn't I tell you?

That was where they lived in Twoland.

Mr Nosey was driving his car back from Happyland.

He had been to see how Mr Happy was, stayed the night, and was now on his way home.

As he was driving along he noticed a signpost he had never seen before.

It was pointing to Twoland.

"Twoland?" he thought to himself. "I've never heard of such a place!"

So, being a nosey fellow, he turned the wheel, and set off to find out where Twoland was.

He's not called Mr Nosey for nothing!

Nosey by name and nosey by nature!

It was a very warm day, and Mr Nosey began to feel decidedly thirsty.

He stopped at the first cottage he came to.

Little Miss Twin was outside, gardening.

"I say," called out Mr Nosey. "Could I possibly trouble you for a glass of water?"

"It's so hot today," he added, apologetically.

"Of course course," smiled little Miss Twin.

"Come on in in!"

Mr Nosey couldn't quite understand why she was talking like that, but he was much too polite to mention the fact.

He got out of his car, and followed little Miss Twin up the garden path of Twotimes Cottage.

"After you you," she said, opening the door for him.

Mr Nosey went in, and jumped.

"I thought you were behind me," he said.

"Oh no no," laughed little Miss Twin. "She's my twin twin!"

"That's right right," giggled the other little Miss Twin behind him.

"Am I in Twoland?" Mr Nosey asked the twins as he sipped his glass of water.

They both giggled.

"Oh yes yes," they said.

"And do you always talk like this?" he asked.

"Like what what?" they said.

"Would you like to stay for lunch lunch?" asked one of the twins.

"It's sausages sausages," added the other.

"How very kind kind," replied Mr Nosey.

Their way of talking seemed to be catching catching!

After lunch the little Miss Twins promised to show Mr Nosey around Twoland.

They took him to the Twotown Art Gallery.

There were two of every painting!

They took him to the Twotown Hall to meet the Mayor.

Mr Doublechin!

"Welcome to our town town," he said as he shook Mr Nosey by the hand.

And then the three of them went for tea to the main hotel in Twotown.

The Ritz Ritz!

They had two cups of tea each and two sandwiches each and two cakes each.

"Let me pay," said Mr Nosey.

"Oh no no," they insisted.

"You're our guest guest," they added.

It was getting quite late when they came out of the Ritz Ritz.

"I really must be going," said Mr Nosey as he climbed into his car, which he had parked outside the hotel. "I don't like driving in the dark!"

"Lovely to meet you Mr Nosey Nosey," said one twin.

"I hope we meet again soon soon," said the other.

"Bye bye," called Mr Nosey as he drove off.

"Bye bye bye," the twins called after him.

Two days later, in Tiddletown, which was where he lived, Mr Nosey received a letter.

It had a Twoland postmark on the envelope.

And two Twoland stamps!

He opened it in great excitement.

Inside the envelope was a parking fine!

For parking his car on a double yellow line outside the Ritz Ritz in Twotown!

Which, as you know, is no place to park park!

3 Great Offers for MR. MEN Fans!

MR. MEN TOKEN

1 New Mr. Men or Little Miss Library Bus Presentation Cases

A brand new stronger, roomier school bus library box, with sturdy carrying handle and stay-closed fasteners.
The full colour, wipe-clean boxes make a great home for your full collection.
They're just £5.99 inc P&P and free bookmark!

☐ MR. MEN ☐ LITTLE MISS (please tick and order overleaf)

2 Door Hangers and Posters

In every Mr. Men and Little Miss book like this one, you will find a special token. Collect 6 tokens and we will send you a brilliant Mr. Men or Little Miss poster and a Mr. Men or Little Miss double sided full colour bedroom door hanger of your choice. Simply tick your choice in the list and tape a 50p coin for your two items to this page.

PLEASE STICK YOUR 50P COIN HERE

Door Hangers (please tick)
☐ Mr. Nosey & Mr. Muddle
☐ Mr. Slow & Mr. Busy
☐ Mr. Messy & Mr. Quiet
☐ Mr. Perfect & Mr. Forgetful
☐ Little Miss Fun & Little Miss Late
☐ Little Miss Helpful & Little Miss Tidy
☐ Little Miss Busy & Little Miss Brainy
☐ Little Miss Star & Little Miss Fun

Posters (please tick)
☐ MR. MEN
☐ LITTLE MISS

3 **Sixteen Beautiful Fridge Magnets –** any **2** for **£2.00!** inc.P&P

They're very special collector's items!
Simply tick your first and second* choices from the list below
of any 2 characters!

1st Choice

- ☐ Mr. Happy
- ☐ Mr. Lazy
- ☐ Mr. Topsy-Turvy
- ☐ Mr. Bounce
- ☐ Mr. Small
- ☐ Mr. Snow
- ☐ Mr. Wrong

- ☐ Mr. Daydream
- ☐ Mr. Tickle
- ☐ Mr. Greedy
- ☐ Mr. Funny
- ☐ Little Miss Giggles
- ☐ Little Miss Splendid
- ☐ Little Miss Naughty
- ☐ Little Miss Sunshine

2nd Choice

- ☐ Mr. Happy
- ☐ Mr. Lazy
- ☐ Mr. Topsy-Turvy
- ☐ Mr. Bounce
- ☐ Mr. Small
- ☐ Mr. Snow
- ☐ Mr. Wrong

- ☐ Mr. Daydream
- ☐ Mr. Tickle
- ☐ Mr. Greedy
- ☐ Mr. Funny
- ☐ Little Miss Giggles
- ☐ Little Miss Splendid
- ☐ Little Miss Naughty
- ☐ Little Miss Sunshine

*Only in case your first choice is out of stock.

--- TO BE COMPLETED BY AN ADULT ---

**To apply for any of these great offers, ask an adult to complete the coupon below and send it with
the appropriate payment and tokens, if needed, to MR. MEN OFFERS, PO BOX 7, MANCHESTER M19 2HD**

☐ Please send ____ Mr. Men Library case(s) and/or ____ Little Miss Library case(s) at £5.99 each inc P&P

☐ Please send a poster and door hanger as selected overleaf. I enclose six tokens plus a 50p coin for P&P

☐ Please send me ____ pair(s) of Mr. Men/Little Miss fridge magnets, as selected above at £2.00 inc P&P

Fan's Name _____

Address _____

_____ **Postcode** _____

Date of Birth _____

Name of Parent/Guardian _____

Total amount enclosed £ _____

☐ **I enclose a cheque/postal order payable to Egmont Books Limited**

☐ **Please charge my MasterCard/Visa/Amex/Switch or Delta account** (delete as appropriate)

| | | | | | | | | | | | | | | | | Card Number

Expiry date ___/___ **Signature** _____

Please allow 28 days for delivery. We reserve the right to change the terms of this offer at any time
but we offer a 14 day money back guarantee. This does not affect your statutory rights.

MR.MEN **LITTLE MISS**
Mr. Men and Little Miss™ & ©Mrs. Roger Hargreaves

CUT ALONG DOTTED LINE AND RETURN THIS WHOLE PAGE